Stories to Grow By

Tunnel 2000
A Tale in Which Edgar Finds Joy in Living

by Kathryn Wheeler
illustrated by Dan Sharp

In Celebration™, Grand Rapids, MI

Library of Congress Cataloging-in-Publication Data

Wheeler, Kathryn, 1954-
    Tunnel 2000 : a tale in which Edgar finds joy in living / by Kathryn Wheeler ;
illustrated by Dan Sharp.
        p. cm. -- (Stories to grow by)
    Summary: Edgar the earthworm hates his job digging tunnels underground until a
rainstorm forces him up to the surface and his friend Esther shows him the importance of
their work. Includes a Bible verse and facts about earthworms.
    ISBN 1-56822-597-0 (hardcover)
    [1. Earthworms--Fiction. 2. Joy--Fiction. 3. Christian life--Fiction.] I. Sharp, Dan, ill.
II. Title. III. Series.

PZ7.W5655 Tu 2000
[E]--dc21
                                                                                    00-022235

Credits
Author: Kathryn Wheeler
Cover and Inside Illustrations: Dan Sharp
Project Director/Editor: Alyson Kieda

ISBN: 1-56822-597-0
Tunnel 2000
Copyright © 1999 by In Celebration®
a division of Instructional Fair Group, Inc.
a Tribune Education Company
3195 Wilson Drive NW
Grand Rapids, Michigan 49544

For information regarding permission write to:
In Celebration®, P.O. Box 1650, Grand Rapids, MI 49501.

Printed in Singapore

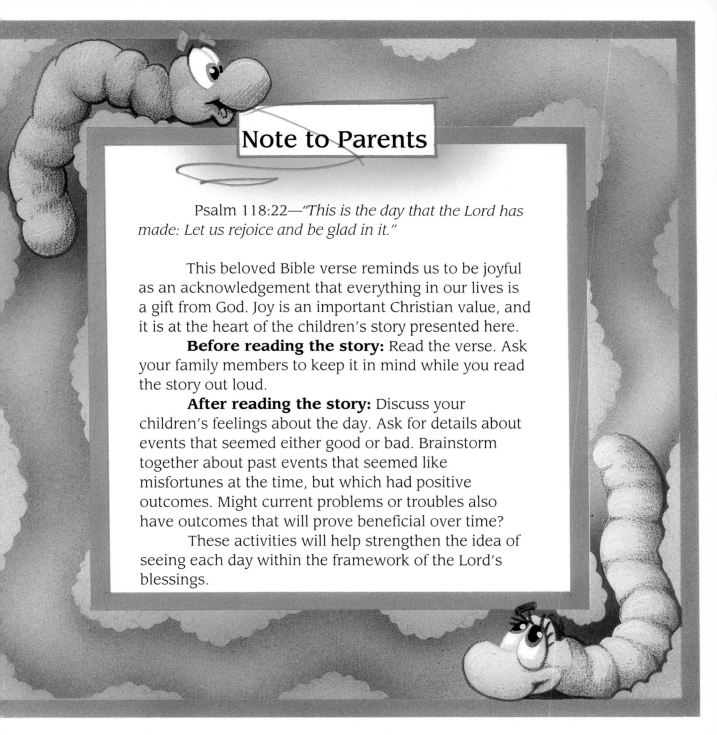

Note to Parents

Psalm 118:22—*"This is the day that the Lord has made: Let us rejoice and be glad in it."*

This beloved Bible verse reminds us to be joyful as an acknowledgement that everything in our lives is a gift from God. Joy is an important Christian value, and it is at the heart of the children's story presented here.

Before reading the story: Read the verse. Ask your family members to keep it in mind while you read the story out loud.

After reading the story: Discuss your children's feelings about the day. Ask for details about events that seemed either good or bad. Brainstorm together about past events that seemed like misfortunes at the time, but which had positive outcomes. Might current problems or troubles also have outcomes that will prove beneficial over time?

These activities will help strengthen the idea of seeing each day within the framework of the Lord's blessings.

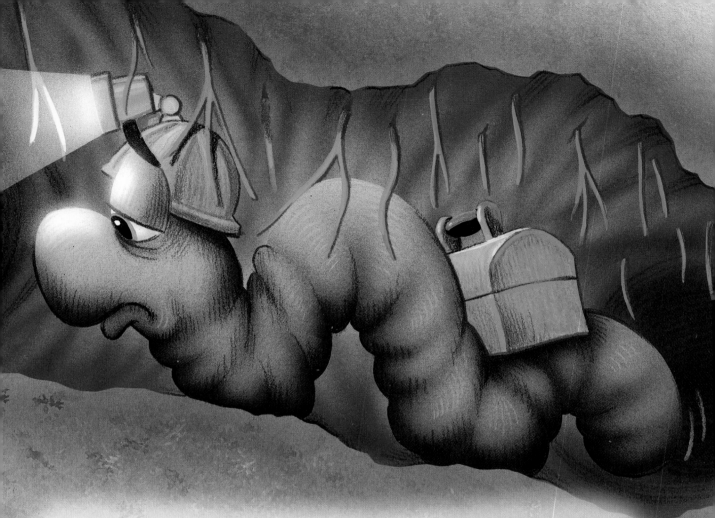

"Another day," sighed Edgar Earthworm as he headed toward Tunnel Number 2000. Edgar inched along, brushing aside roots that dangled in his way. "I hate these roots," he muttered. Guided by the light on his miner's hat, Edgar turned into his tunnel. He prodded a clammy lump of clay. "I hate this clay," grumbled Edgar. "I hate these tunnels. And I hate this job."

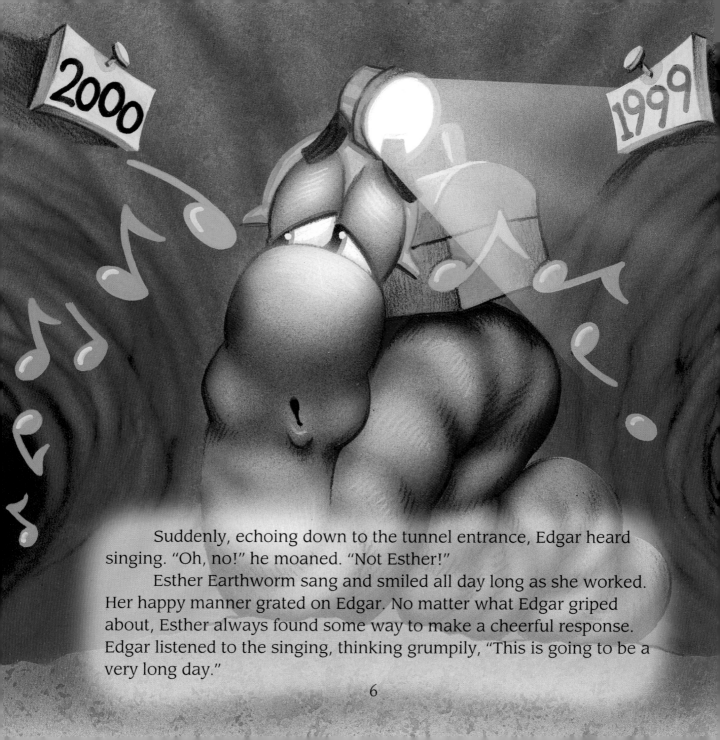

Suddenly, echoing down to the tunnel entrance, Edgar heard singing. "Oh, no!" he moaned. "Not Esther!"

Esther Earthworm sang and smiled all day long as she worked. Her happy manner grated on Edgar. No matter what Edgar griped about, Esther always found some way to make a cheerful response. Edgar listened to the singing, thinking grumpily, "This is going to be a very long day."

"Hello, there, Edgar! Glad to see you!" said a happy voice. "Isn't it a great day?"

"Hi, Esther," said Edgar. "Actually, I'm already tired of Tunnel 2000. In fact, what I'd really like is a day off."

"But, Edgar, we have such important work to do here!" Esther hummed as she rolled some clay aside and began cleaning the dirt off some dangling roots.

Edgar sighed. "Right, Esther. We move dirt from one place to another. Very important."

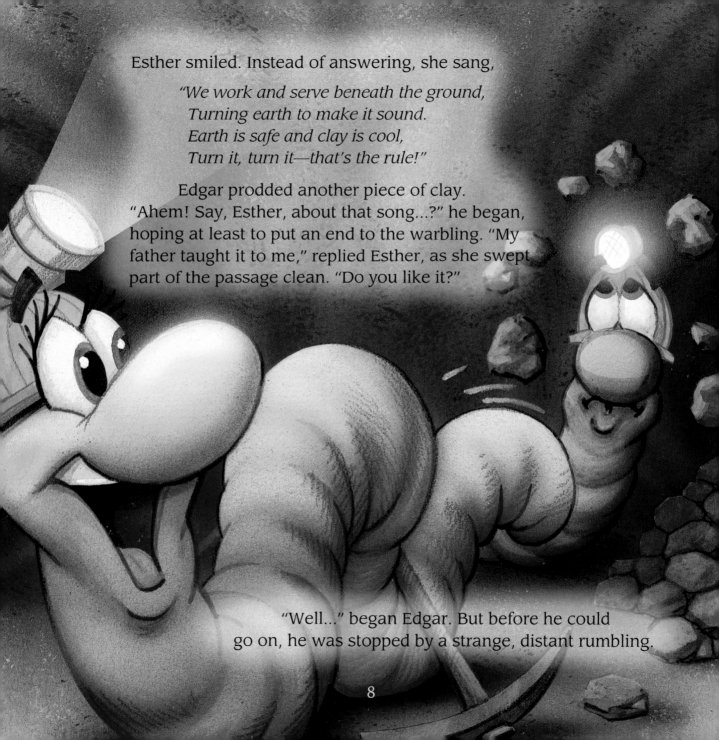

Esther smiled. Instead of answering, she sang,

> *"We work and serve beneath the ground,*
> *Turning earth to make it sound.*
> *Earth is safe and clay is cool,*
> *Turn it, turn it—that's the rule!"*

Edgar prodded another piece of clay. "Ahem! Say, Esther, about that song...?" he began, hoping at least to put an end to the warbling. "My father taught it to me," replied Esther, as she swept part of the passage clean. "Do you like it?"

"Well..." began Edgar. But before he could go on, he was stopped by a strange, distant rumbling.

Esther dropped her pick and raised her head.

"What is that noise?" Edgar said. Another rumble, echoing down the tunnel, made Esther gasp.

"Run!" she cried to Edgar. "That's thunder! Head for the surface!"

"But we're not supposed to go up there," Edgar reminded her.

"Run!" cried Esther, as she began burrowing straight through the tunnel ceiling. Edgar's ears were filled with a loud whoosh, and before he could even blink, he was underwater!

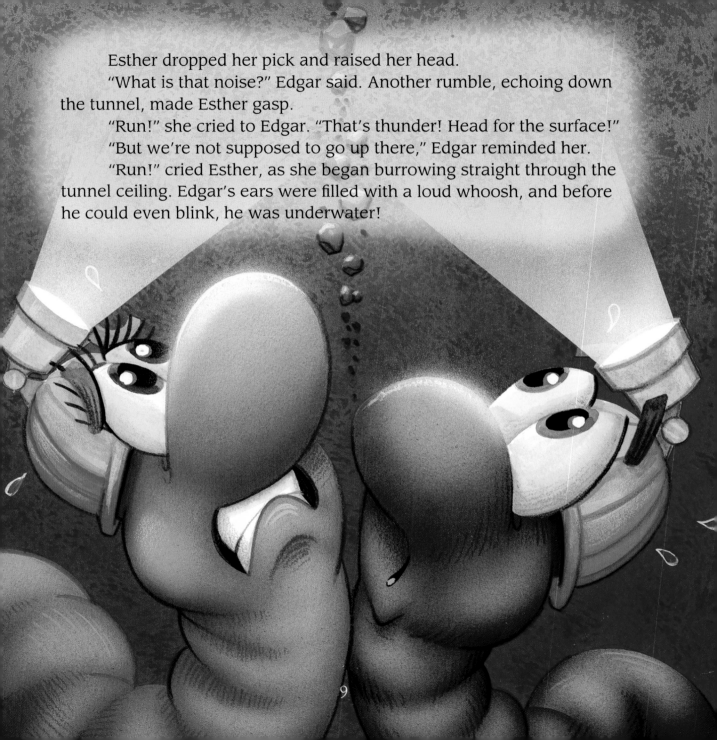

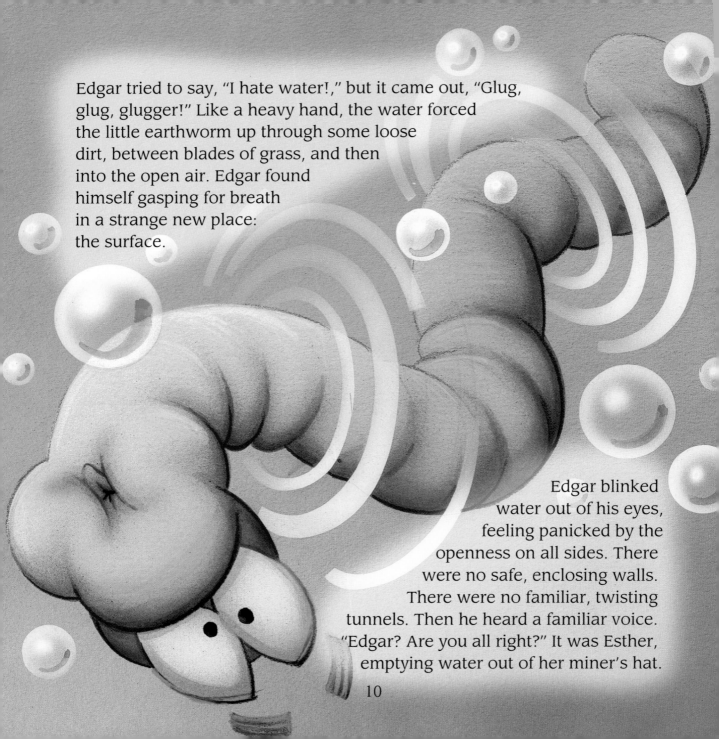

Edgar tried to say, "I hate water!," but it came out, "Glug, glug, glugger!" Like a heavy hand, the water forced the little earthworm up through some loose dirt, between blades of grass, and then into the open air. Edgar found himself gasping for breath in a strange new place: the surface.

Edgar blinked water out of his eyes, feeling panicked by the openness on all sides. There were no safe, enclosing walls. There were no familiar, twisting tunnels. Then he heard a familiar voice. "Edgar? Are you all right?" It was Esther, emptying water out of her miner's hat.

10

"What's happening?" sputtered Edgar.

"This is rain," said Esther. "It fills the tunnels with water and forces us up to the surface. You learn these things when you've been on the job as long as I have."

"We could have drowned!" cried Edgar.

Esther smiled. "I know. Aren't we lucky?" Before Edgar could answer, Esther peered at the vast, grey sky. "We have to be careful, though, because we don't want to get eaten by a..."

Edgar heard another whoosh. But this time, the sound was the beating of wings. A set of sharp claws closed around Edgar's body.

11

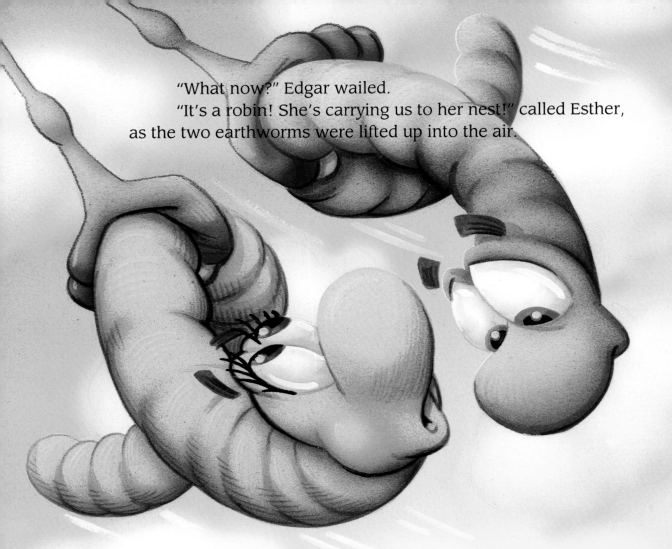

"What now?" Edgar wailed.

"It's a robin! She's carrying us to her nest!" called Esther, as the two earthworms were lifted up into the air.

"Heeeellllppp!!!" screamed Edgar.

"Wriggle!" Esther shouted. "We have to slip out of her grasp!"

Edgar was already wriggling and struggling in the robin's grasp. Just as he was nearly free, he looked down and saw the comforting ground far below. Edgar shut his eyes and went completely limp.

12

Edgar came to as he thudded back onto the grass.
Esther landed beside him.

"What a fall! Our backs could have been broken!" Edgar moaned.

"Good thing we don't have spines!" Esther answered
cheerfully. "Hurry, let's get undercover. Head for that hedge over there."

13

When at last Edgar peered out from underneath the hedge's lowest branches, he saw another strange sight: a blur of bright colors. Tall and low, yellow and red and pink and blue, the shapes billowed like bright clouds balanced on top of giant blades of grass.

"What are those?" he asked in hushed tones.

"Those are flowers," Esther answered happily. "That's what we help to make."

"We do? I thought we just moved dirt around." Edgar felt confused.

"We turn the earth and make tunnels for the roots of the flowers," answered Esther. "That helps the flowers grow strong, so they can bloom. Look, see those flowers over there?" She pointed at a bunch of straggly stems with pink buds. "Those are the flowers above Tunnel 2000. They need our help. That's why we're working there."

Edgar gazed at the pink flowers. They needed his help! He felt his heart beating fast. "We have to get back to work right now!" he announced, inching out toward the grass.

Esther grabbed Edgar's tail. "Hold on!" she said. "First we have to wait until the sun dries out our tunnels. You don't want to go scuba diving again, do you?" Esther looked around. "Hey, look!" she said. "Here's an apple core. What a feast!" She broke off part of the fruit and handed it to Edgar.

16

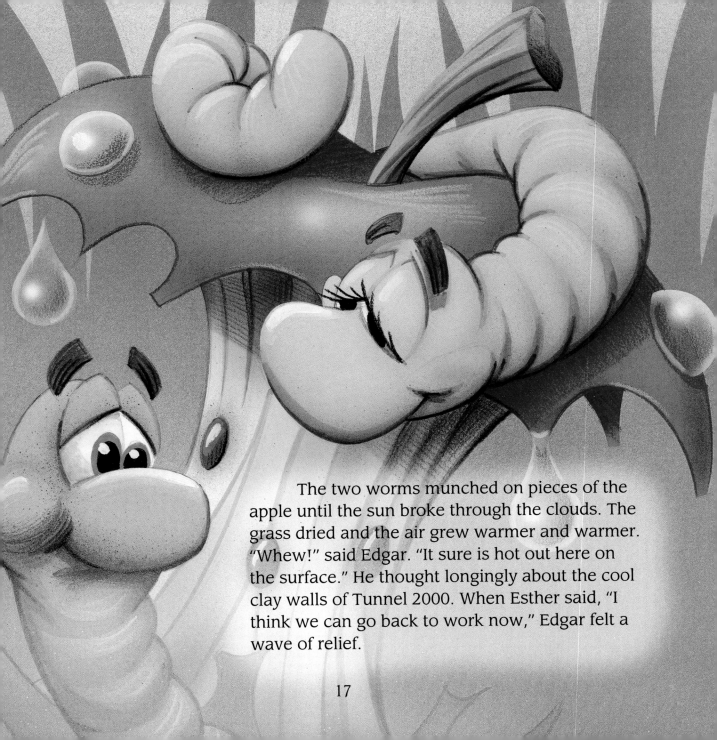

The two worms munched on pieces of the apple until the sun broke through the clouds. The grass dried and the air grew warmer and warmer. "Whew!" said Edgar. "It sure is hot out here on the surface." He thought longingly about the cool clay walls of Tunnel 2000. When Esther said, "I think we can go back to work now," Edgar felt a wave of relief.

As the earthworms burrowed their way into their tunnel, Esther said, "Well, you got your wish. A day off!"

Edgar grinned. "If that's what a vacation is like, I'll take work any day!" he replied. As they turned into the entrance of Tunnel 2000, Edgar said energetically, "Okay, Esther. You start clearing the clay out of the center section, and I'll clean off these roots. We have to hurry. We have important work to do!"

As Esther headed down the tunnel, Edgar called her back. "Uh, say, Esther...think you could teach me that song of yours?"

Esther smiled. "I'd love to," she answered.

A Note About Earthworms

Earthworms can be found all over the world, wherever there is moist, warm soil for them to tunnel through. They have flexible bodies that are constructed like an inner and outer tube. The inner tube contains their brain, digestive track, and other organs. Worms do not have eyes or ears, but they can sense light and heat and can feel touch.

Worms do not have lungs. They breathe through their thin, sensitive skin and depend on the air in their tunnels and between dirt particles. When it rains, these air pockets fill up with water. That's why worms must come to the surface of the earth when it rains. If they don't, they risk drowning.

Earthworms help break down the soil as they eat dead plant material and move through the earth, creating passages which allow air movement to reach plant roots. Plant growth is greatly aided by the tunneling of earthworms, and in areas where worms do not live, some plants have a more difficult time growing and thriving.

Earthworms come in all sizes: some grow to be 11 feet long! All of them, regardless of size, have a complex muscle system which allows them to stretch out or shrink in size.